STEP-by-STEP

SCIENCE

Color

Robert Snedden and Sabrina Crewe

Illustrated by Stuart Lafford,
Raymond Turvey and Joanna Williams

CHILDREN'S PRESS®

A Division of Grolier Publishing

NEW YORK • LONDON • HONG KONG • SYDNEY
DANBURY, CONNECTICUT

Photographs: Bridgeman Art Library/Musee de l'Orangerie, Paris/Lauros-Giraudon (Claude Monet **Argenteuil** 1872-5); Bruce Coleman: page 5 right (Kevin Burchett), 19 top (Michael McCoy), 21 (Andy Purcell), 22 top (Jane Burton), 22 bottom (Konrad Wothe), 23 top (Joe McDonald), 23 bottom (C C Lockwood); Getty Images: page 6 (Andy Sacks), 17 top (Lori Adamski Peek), 18 (Bruce Forster), 26 (Gary Yeowell), 29 (Michael Scott); Robert Harding Picture Library: page 11, 14, 17 bottom, 24; The Image Bank: page 4 (Terje Rakke), 5 (left) (Jeff Hunter), 7 (Weinberg/Clark), 12 (right), 19 (Bottom) (Grant V Faint), 29 bottom (Don Landwehrle); Oxford Scientific Films: page 31 bottom (Alastair Shay); Redferns Music Picture Library: page 31 top (S Morley); Science Photo Library: page 25 both (C Nuridsany/M Perennou); Spectrum Colour Library: page 12 left, ZEFA: cover.

Planning and production by Discovery Books Limited
Designed by Ian Winton
Edited by Helena Attlee
Consultant: Jeremy Bloomfield

Visit Children's Press on the Internet at:
http://publishing.grolier.com

First published in 1998 by Franklin Watts

First American edition 1998 by Children's Press

ISBN: 0-516-20956-6
A CIP catalog record
for this book is available from
the Library of Congress

J
536.6
SNE

Printed in Dubai

Contents

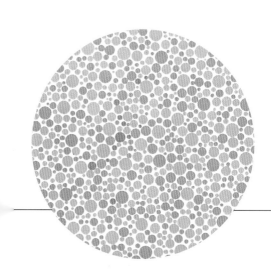

A Colorful World

Imagine a world without color. These colorful sailboats would seem quite different...

...if they were in black and white.

We use color all the time to describe things and to tell them apart. We use colors to paint imaginary worlds of our own. The colors of nature make the real world a beautiful place.

We are lucky to live in a very colorful world. Bright colors make us feel happy. We can use colors to cheer ourselves up on a gray day.

Primary Colors

When you paint a picture, you may want to use many colors. You can make hundreds of colors by mixing different paints together.

There are three colors you need to make all other colors. Red, yellow, and blue are called **primary colors**. Primary colors can't be made by mixing other colors. But if you have red, yellow, and blue, you can make all the colors you want!

Mixing Colors

What happens when you mix blue with yellow? You make green. Green isn't a primary color, so you have to mix other colors to make it. Mixing yellow with red makes orange. Mixing red with blue makes purple. What happens if you mix many colors together?

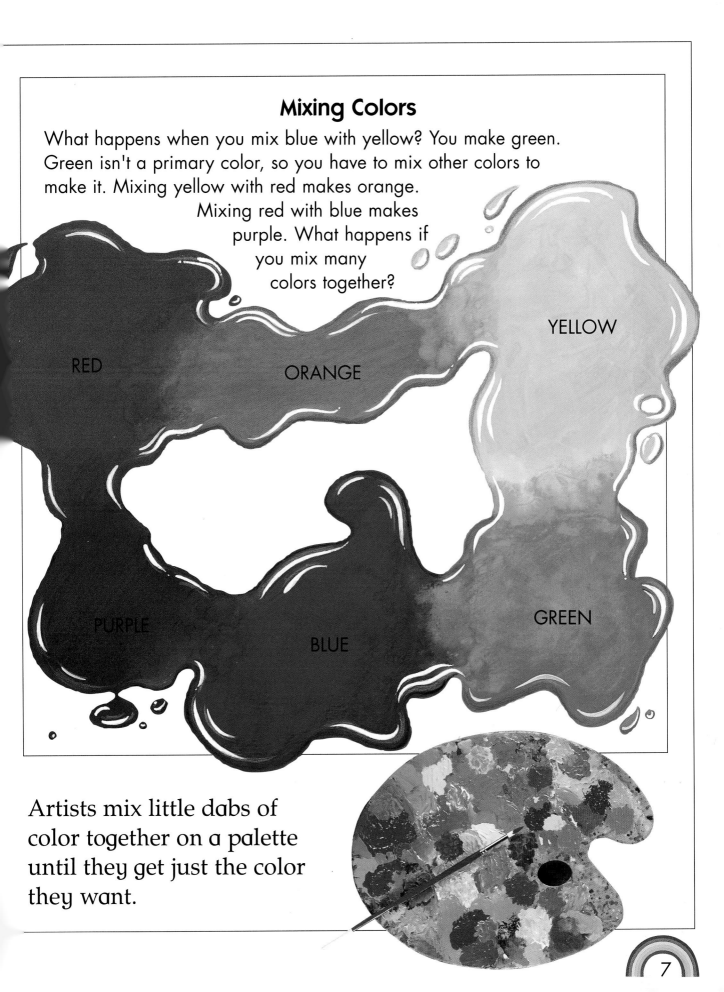

RED

ORANGE

YELLOW

PURPLE

BLUE

GREEN

Artists mix little dabs of color together on a palette until they get just the color they want.

Shades of Color

When you make a paint paler or darker, you are changing its **shade**. To make colors paler, you must add white. Blue becomes pale blue. Red becomes pink. If you want to change a color to a darker shade, you must add black.

Red	Pink	White

MAKING SHADES

You can make a shade chart by choosing a color and making it darker and lighter. You will need poster paints in black, white, and one other color, such as a bright blue.

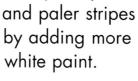

1. Put two blobs of blue paint on a plate. Now paint a stripe down the middle of a piece of paper.

2. Add a few drops of white to your blue paint and mix it in. Paint a paler stripe to the left of your first one. Continue to paint paler and paler stripes by adding more white paint.

3. Now add a tiny bit of black to your other blob of blue paint. Paint a darker stripe to the right of the first one. Add more black to make even darker stripes.

Painters use light and dark shades of many colors in one painting. When you look from far away, you see the colors all blended together. When you look up close, you can see tiny brushstrokes in different shades and colors.

Pigments

The tiny pieces of color used to make paints are called **pigments**. Many pigments come from plants and animals. Others come from rocks. Long ago, these natural pigments were the only colors people had.

Natural pigments usually make soft, rich colors. Many of the bright colors we have today are not natural. They are made from **chemicals**.

Thousands of years ago, the first artists used natural pigments to paint animals on the walls of caves. The cave painters made their paint by grinding up colored rocks and charcoal. They used twigs, leaves, and blowpipes to paint the mixture on the walls.

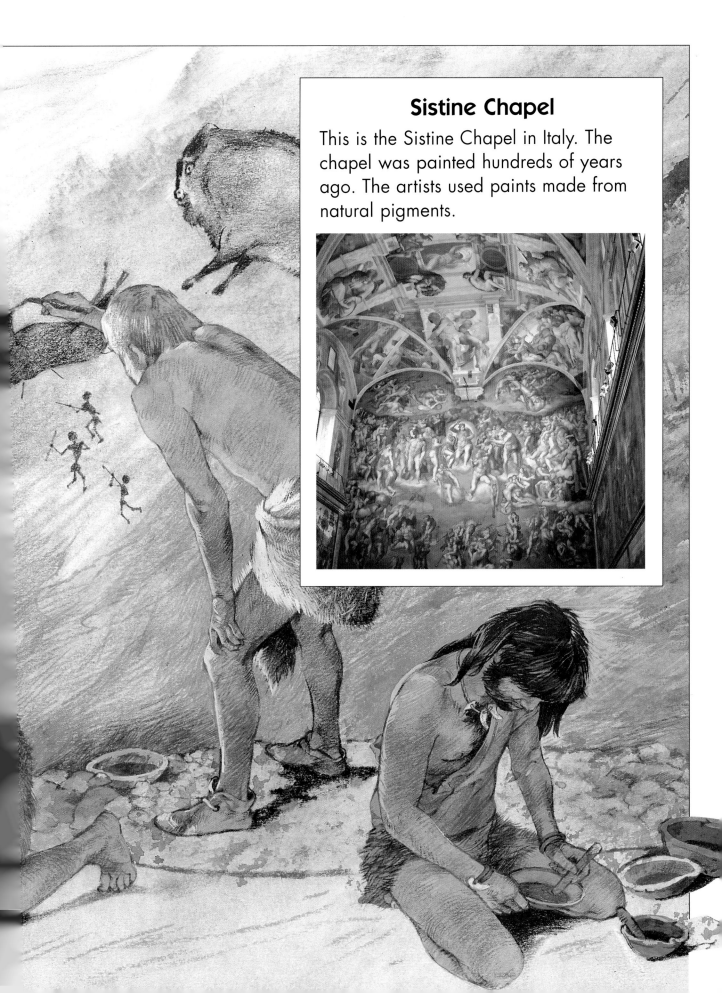

Sistine Chapel

This is the Sistine Chapel in Italy. The chapel was painted hundreds of years ago. The artists used paints made from natural pigments.

Making Dyes

Dyes are used to color things when the color needs to last. People use dyes for coloring clothes, paper, and food.

All paints used to be made from plant juices, shellfish, insects, and other natural materials.

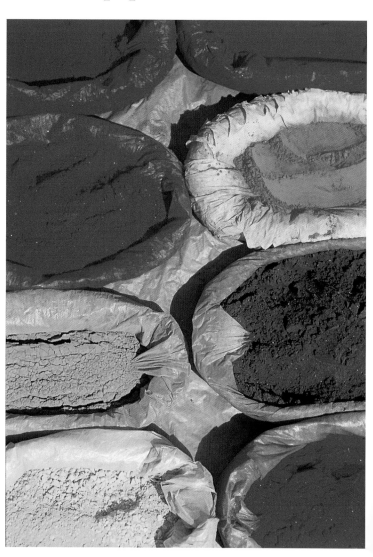

Today most dyes are made from chemicals. Chemical dyes make many bright colors for clothes and other things.

VEGETABLE COLORS

You can make your own vegetable dyes and use them to dye a piece of white fabric, such as an old T-shirt or handkerchief. You can use onion skins, which will give you a yellow dye, or beet, which will give you a pink dye.

1. Ask an adult to boil some onion skins or beets with a little water in an old saucepan. The mixture should simmer for about fifteen minutes.

2. Leave the mixture to cool. Ask your adult helper to pour the colored liquid through a strainer into a bowl.

3. Take a piece of fabric and put it into the bowl. Make sure all the fabric gets soaked in the dye.

4. After the fabric has soaked for a few minutes, take it out of the bowl and squeeze it out. Then hang it up to dry.

Color Power

How do colors make you feel? What do they make you think of? A brightly colored room will create a different mood from a room painted in pale, cool colors.

Moody Colors

Green makes us think of leaves and trees in cool, shady places. It can make people feel relaxed.

Blue is a cold color. It makes us think of water and ice.

Some colors grab your attention. When yellow and black are used together, they are very easy to see. That's why these colors are often used on roads. It is very important that drivers notice them.

Red is also easy to see. Many warning signs are colored red to help people spot them. If a red flag is flying on a beach, people can see from a distance that it is not safe to swim.

Red is the color of hot things, and it makes us think of danger and excitement.

Yellow is a sunny color. It makes us feel warm.

Colorful Messages

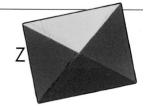

Colors are very useful for sending signals. Messages using colored lights or flags can be understood all over the world. In many countries, traffic lights flash red for "stop" and green for "go."

A

B

C

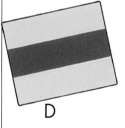

D

E

Colored lights are used by airplanes at night. Airplanes have red lights on the left wing, green lights on the right wing, and white lights on the tail. This shows pilots where other airplanes are and which way they are going.

F

G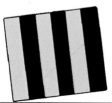

H

I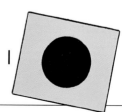

J

Y X W V U T S R Q P

Bright colors are used in sports so that people can easily tell their teams apart.

Flags are flown on ships to send signals. The different colors and shapes on the flags spell out messages.

Each flag stands for a different letter of the alphabet. Can you find the letters of your name?

L M N O

People Colors

Have you ever wondered why people have different skin, hair, and eye colors? It has to do with different amounts of pigment. Skin, hair, and eyes get their colors from pigment in our bodies.

Everybody's skin is the same, except that pale skin has less pigment in it than dark skin. Different amounts of pigment can make all hair colors, from pale blonde and red to black.

Blue

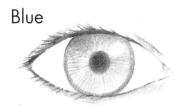

Green

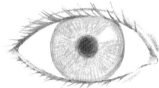

Brown

People have always used colors to decorate their skin and dye their hair.

This man from Papua New Guinea has painted his face in a traditional way.

Sometimes people paint their faces just for fun.

Animal Colors

Many animals are brightly colored. Sometimes their colors warn other animals that they are poisonous or can sting.

Some birds are very brightly colored. Male birds are usually brighter than females. Males sit where they can easily be seen, showing their colored feathers. They do this to protect their **territory**. Male birds also **attract** female birds with their bright colors.

Some animals use bright colors to confuse their **predators**. If approached by a hungry bird, the red underwing moth shows its red and black underwings to frighten the bird away.

Camouflage

Some animals are hard to see. The colors of their skin or the patterns on their fur match their surroundings. This is called **camouflage**. Camouflage helps protect many animals from predators.

Chameleons can change their color to match their background.

The stripes of a tiger look striking out in the open. But the tiger blends well with the light and shade in long grass. This helps the tiger hunt other animals.

People sometimes use camouflage, too. Soldiers camouflage themselves to hide from enemies.

This mountain hare is brown in the summer, but in the winter it grows a new white coat to help it hide against the snow.

Flower Colors

Flowers come in many bright colors. These colors attract insects, who go to flowers to collect nectar and pollen. When they do this, they help the flowers make seeds.

Some flowers have special pigments that people can't see. These pigments make colors that can only be seen in **ultraviolet** light. Because bees and other insects use ultraviolet light to see, they can see colors that are invisible to us.

Bee's-Eye View

The photograph on the left shows how a potentilla flower looks to us.

The special photograph on the right shows us what it would look like to a bee. The dark patches on the petals show bees and other insects the way to the flower's nectar.

Plants that are visited by moths often have white flowers. Moths look for their food at night, and white shows up in the dark better than other colors.

Rainbows

Have you ever seen a rainbow in the sky when it is raining? Where do you think the colors come from?

Sunlight looks white, but it contains light of many colors. When it rains, sunlight hits the raindrops. The light bends and splits into separate bands of color. These are the colors you see when you look at a rainbow.

The colors you see in a rainbow are called the colors of the **spectrum**. When raindrops bend sunlight, some of the colors bend more than others. Red bends the most. Violet bends the least. That's why we see them as separate bands.

Red

Orange

Yellow

Green

Blue

Violet

MAKE A RAINBOW SPINNER

You can mix the colors of the spectrum back together to make white.

1. Cut out a circle about 6 in (15 cm) across from white cardboard.

2. Make a rainbow disk by coloring your circle with the colors of the spectrum. Use colored pencils so that your colors are pale.

3. Ask an adult to make a hole in the middle of the cardboard. Push a pencil through the hole to make a spinning disk.

4. Spin the rainbow disk as fast as you can. What happens to the colors?

Seeing Colors

Sunlight contains light of many colors. When sunlight shines on an object, some colors in the light are **absorbed** and others are reflected. The reflected light bounces off the object and into our eyes. The color of the reflected light is the color we see.

Animal Vision

Many animals see the world with very little color. They see mostly in black, white, and gray.

A strawberry reflects red light, so we see it as red. The leaves of a plant reflect green light, so we see them as green. The colors reflected by different things depend on what the things are made of.

Color Blindness

People who are color blind have trouble seeing colors. They may not be able to tell red from green. Look at this pattern of colored spots. Can you see a number in the pattern? A color-blind person could not see it because the colors would all look the same.

The parts of our eyes that pick up colors don't work in the dark. If there is a little bit of light, we can still see shapes and objects but not their colors.

Color Filters

If you look through a colored piece of cellophane, the colors you see will seem strange. A colored sheet of plastic, glass, or cellophane only lets through light that is the same color as itself. It is acting as a **filter**.

A green filter will only let through green light. If you look at a red object through a green filter, it will appear black.

FILTER FUN

You can have fun making your own colored filters.

1. Find some colored cellophane or plastic, such as candy wrappers.

2. Draw a rainbow and then look at it through your different-colored filters. Can you still see all the rainbow's colors each time?

3. Look at other things through your filters and see if their colors have changed.

4. Put your filters over a flashlight to make different-colored lights. Shine your flashlight on the wall and see how the filters change the color of the light.

Spotlights using different filters can make wonderful colors appear on a stage.

The sunlight comes into this church through a stained-glass window. Each piece of different-colored glass only lets through light of its own color.

Glossary

Absorbed: When the colors in light are taken in by an object instead of reflected, we say that they have been absorbed.

Attract: To get the attention of another person or animal.

Camouflage: Colors or markings that blend in with the background and help hide animals or objects.

Chemicals: The many substances that mix together in different ways to make all living and non-living things.

Filter: Something that only lets through some of the colors in light. The colors that pass through depend on the color of the filter itself.

Pigments: Colored substances that give color to other things.

Predators: Animals that hunt and kill other animals for food.

Primary colors: Colors that cannot be made by mixing other colors but can be used to make other colors.

Shade: Darker and lighter versions of the same color.

Spectrum: The spread of colors that can be seen when white light is split up.

Territory: The area that an animal defends as its own.

Ultraviolet: A part of the light spectrum that comes after violet and can't be seen by people.

Index